BIG BAD DOG

Pictures by Sally Holmes

Lucy had a kitten called Cuddle. You can guess why she called it Cuddle – because it was so cuddlesome! It was black all over except for a white shirt-front which Cuddle kept very, very clean.

"In fact, you keep it so clean, Cuddle, that I almost believe you send it to the laundry!" said Lucy, hugging her kitten.

Cuddle was pretty and loving – but oh, so naughty! She pulled all the flowers out of the vases. She knocked over the milk-jug on the table. She broke a lamp when she chased a fly, and she sent all the fire-irons clattering down when she tried to get her ball from the fireplace.

"I hope that kitten will soon settle
down and be good," said Lucy's
mother. "It really is very naughty,
and if it breaks any more things I shall
get cross with it."
"Well, Mummy, it isn't so naughty as
the big bad dog next door," said Lucy.
"No – I suppose it isn't," said
Mummy. "It is really a very bad dog.
It broke Daddy's Michaelmas daisies
down yesterday – and it uprooted all
the bulbs he planted."

Daniel was certainly a very bad dog. He was a Great Dane. He was almost as big as Lucy. Lucy liked him for although he was naughty, he was gentle and sweet with her, and never rough. But his great big feet spoilt the garden when they tramped on it, and Mummy had to see that there was no meat, fish or cakes left about if he came in, for he put his great paws up on table or shelf and gobbled everything!

Daniel lived next door. There was wire between the gardens so that he could not get through – but there was one place where he could jump right over, and that was how he came in. He was fond of Lucy and often came to find her.

"What with that naughty little kitten and that big bad dog I really am worried to death!" said Mummy, shooing Daniel out of the kitchen. "Shoo, Daniel, shoo! Will you *please* stop sniffing at the larder door. Your dinner is NOT in there!"
Daniel shooed. He leapt over the wire and trotted back to his own house. Then Cuddle the kitten, who had hidden behind a chair when Daniel walked in, came out to look around. Cuddle was afraid of the big dog. It seemed like an elephant to her.

Cuddle spied a bowl of goldfish on the dining-room bookcase when she wandered into that room. She climbed up and looked down into the bowl. What was this bright red thing that glided in and out so quickly? She put in her paw and tried to catch the fish. But when she took her paw out, it was wet and cold. Cuddle didn't like it. She tried to jump over the bowl to get down the way she got up – but she hit the bowl and it fell over! Down, down, down it went – and crash, splash, it was on the floor, broken and spilt! The goldfish wriggled and gasped.

Mummy and Lucy ran in. They put
the goldfish into a dish of water and
cleared up the mess. "That was very,
very naughty of you, Cuddle," said
Mummy crossly.

Cuddle went into a corner and licked
her wet paw. Then she thought she
would see what was up the chimney.
So she went to the empty fireplace and
peeped up. She gave a spring and
began to scramble up. Down came a
whole pile of soot on to the hearth!

Cuddle fell with it – and goodness me, she had no white shirt-front now! She was covered with black soot! She ran to the sofa, jumped up on to a cushion, and began to wash herself.

What a mess there was when Mummy came into the room! Soot all over the place – and the sofa and cushion quite black where Cuddle had walked and sat and washed. Mummy called Lucy. "Now look, Lucy," she said, "your kitten has been very tiresome again. You must think of somebody else to give it to. I really can't have it behaving like this. If it would only do a *good* thing sometimes instead of being so bad – but it never does. It's just naughty, naughty, naughty all day long!"

Lucy began to cry. She loved Cuddle. "Oh, Mummy, let me keep Cuddle," she begged. "I am sure she will be good soon."

But Mummy said no, Cuddle must go to some other home. She really was too naughty to keep.

Now that night Mummy was going to have Uncle Jim, Auntie Jane, and Granny to supper, so she had quite a lot of cooking to do. She had two nice

chickens roasting, potatoes,
cauliflower and bread sauce, and a big
trifle. Lucy thought it all looked
lovely. She wasn't going to stay up to
supper, but she wanted to see
everything on the table.

Supper was at a quarter to eight. It was Granny's birthday, which was why there was to be a party. Mummy was very anxious that everthing should be nice for Granny. She made Lucy shut Cuddle up in her bedroom in case the kitten tripped her up as she was carrying dishes into the dining-room.

Granny and Uncle Jim and Auntie Jane arrived. They sat in the drawing-room talking to Daddy, whilst Mummy got the supper ready. She carried the roast chickens to the table. She went out to get the vegetables, and Lucy went to help her.

Now Cuddle smelt the dinner cooking and she badly wanted to go and see what was happening. She scraped at the door but it wouldn't open. So she went to the window. It was open at the top. It didn't take Cuddle long to jump up to the top, slide down the glass, spring to the window-sill, get down the tree outside and go into the dining-room, where a delicious smell hung about.

"Whatever is making that glorious smell?" wondered Cuddle. She jumped up on to the table and saw the chickens – and just at that very moment who should walk in at the dining-room door but the very big bad dog, Daniel!

He too had smelt the good smell, and had at once jumped over the wire to come and see what it was. He had trotted in at the garden door unseen – and there he was in the dining-room! Cuddle stared at him in fright. Whatever was she to do? How could she escape? If she jumped off the table the big bad dog would get her! And he would get her if she stayed there too – for already he had put his enormous paws up on the tablecloth and was sniff-sniff-sniffing as hard as ever he could.

Now hanging down over the table was the bell-pull. If Mummy had had a maid she could have rung this bell for the maid to come and clear the table. The bell-pull hung on a long cream wire, and when it was tugged, the bell rang loudly in the kitchen. Well, poor little Cuddle saw this bell-pull and thought that perhaps if she jumped up on it she would be safe from that hungry looking dog.

If she had only known it, Daniel wasn't sniffing for her at all! He was

sniffing at the two roast chickens. He
had never smelt anything so good in
his life!

He put his nose as near as he could to
them, meaning to lick them, and then
to pick them up and run off with them.
Cuddle gave a howl of fright. She
jumped straight up to the bell-pull and
hung there, clutching with all her
claws at the cream wire. The bell at
once rang loudly in the kitchen. Jingle-
jang-jang, jingle-jang-jang!

Daniel got a shock when the kitten jumped high like that. He stared at her swinging on the bell-pull and then began to sniff at the chickens again. Cuddle hung on the bell-pull and swung to and fro. The bell went on ringing loudly in the kitchen Jingle-jang-jang, jingle-jang-jang, Jingle-jang-jang!

Mummy and Lucy were most astonished. "Somebody's ringing and ringing the dining-room bell – quick, who is it?" cried Mummy, and she and Lucy rushed into the dining-room. And there they saw Daniel just about to take a roast chicken in his enormous mouth, and Cuddle the kitten hanging valiantly on to the bell-pull, whilst it rang and rang and rang!

"Bad dog, bad dog!" cried Mummy, and she rushed at Daniel who ran straight out of the door, jumped over the wire and went home! Cuddle dropped down to the table and mewed pitifully. She was very frightened.

"Oh, you clever little kitten! You saw that that big bad dog was going to steal the supper, and you rang the bell to warn us!" cried Lucy, picking Cuddle up and hugging her.

"Mummy, isn't she clever? She saved the chickens!"

Everyone came in to see what all the excitement was about – and when

Granny heard about it, she said, "Well, well, what a clever kitten! Surely, surely you won't give it away now, will you? After all, it isn't every kitten that can do a thing like that! As it is my birthday I shall ask a birthday wish – please let Lucy keep that clever little kitten!"

"Very well," said Mother, laughing.
"I must grant your birthday wish,
Granny. But I just wonder whether
Cuddle was as clever as we think!"
"Of course she was!" said Granny.
"Come along, kitty dear – you shall be
on my knee at supper-time and have a
bit of chicken for a reward!"

So Cuddle had a fine time – and the funny thing was that she turned over a new leaf after that, and was never very naughty again. As for Daniel, the wire was made higher still, and now he can't possibly jump over it. So the big bad dog doesn't come into the garden any more, and Cuddle is very pleased!